WHICH HORSE IS WILLIAM?

by Karla Kuskin

Greenwillow Books, New York

The art was preseparated by the artist
in three colors, red, yellow, and black.
The text type is Esprit Book.

Copyright © 1959, renewed 1987, by Karla Kuskin
Additional artwork copyright © 1992 by Karla Kuskin
First published in 1959 by Harper & Row, Publishers.
New, revised edition published in 1992 by Greenwillow Books.

Library of Congress Cataloging-in-Publication Data
Kuskin, Karla.
     Which horse is William?/by Karla Kuskin
     p. cm.
     "First published in 1959 by Harper & Row Publishers"
     — T.p. verso.
     Summary: William's mother knows him so well that she
can distinguish him from everyone else in the world—
even if he were a horse or a songbird or a mouse or a pig.
     ISBN 0-688-10637-4 (trade).
     ISBN 0-688-10638-2 (lib.)
     [1. Individuality—Fiction.] I. Title.
PZ7.K965Wh   1992   [E]—dc20
90-24619   CIP   AC

FOR WILLIAM

WILLIAM SHORT's mother, Mrs. Short, knew him very well. She knew that he had light brown hair, dark blue eyes, and sneakers. Mrs. Short could tell the sound of William's footsteps when he walked by outside, and she could tell the sound of William's voice from far away.

"Can you tell me from everyone else in the world?" William Short asked his mother.

"Certainly," said Mrs. Short, as she put something in the oven.

"If I were a horse, would you know it was me?" William Short asked his mother.

"Of course," said Mrs. Short.

William Short walked to the field where the horses played,
and he turned into a horse and galloped over the field,
neighing and playing.

"I see you, William, dear," said his mother. "You're the only
horse with a hat on."

"That's me," said William Short, and he stomped his hoofs.

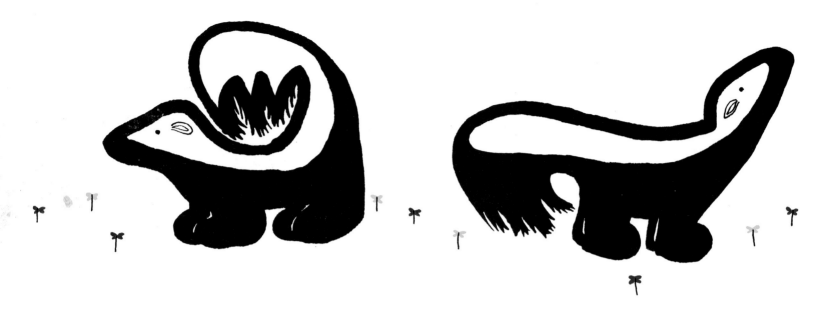

Out among the field flowers the skunks meandered.

"If I were a skunk, would you know it was me?" William Short asked his mother.

"Without a doubt," said Mrs. Short.

So William turned into a skunk and dawdled and dallied with the other skunks.

"I see you, William, dear," said his mother. "You're the only skunk with a scarf on."

"That's me," said William Short, and he swallowed a field flower.

Down in the valley the lambs rambled and gamboled.

"If I were a lamb, would you know it was me?" William Short
asked his mother.

"Indeed," said Mrs. Short.

So William turned into a lamb and rolled in the grass with the
other lambs.

"I see you, William, dear," said his mother. "You're the only
lamb wearing a bright red sweater."

"That's me," said William Short, and he waggled his woolen tail.

At the edge of the pond the ducks were quacking.

"If I were a duck, would you know it was me?" William Short
asked his mother.

"Doubtless," said Mrs. Short.

So William turned into a duck and crashed and splashed at
the edge of the pond.

"I see you, William, dear," said his mother. "You're the only
duck wearing cowboy boots."

"That's me," said William Short, and he paddled around
the pond.

Beside the barn the mice were squeaking.

"If I were a mouse, would you know it was me?" William Short
asked his mother.

"Absolutely," said Mrs. Short.

So William turned into a mouse and squeaked and peeped
with the other mice.

"I see you, William, dear," said his mother. "You're the only
mouse with mittens on."

"That's me," said William Short, and he whiffled his whiskers.

Above the green and grassy lawn the songbirds circled.
"If I were a songbird, would you know it was me?" William
Short asked his mother.
"Positively," said Mrs. Short.
So William turned into a songbird and twittered and flew
through bushes and trees.
"I see you, William, dear," said his mother. "You're the only
songbird standing on his head."
"That's me," said William Short, and he sang a long song.

Under a tree the rabbits ran races.

"If I were a rabbit, would you know it was me?" William
Short asked his mother.

"Oh, my, yes," said Mrs. Short.

So William turned into a rabbit and flounced and pounced
with the other rabbits.

"I see you, William, dear," his mother said. "You're the only
rabbit on roller skates."

"That's me," said William Short, and he wiggled his ears.

Alongside the river the dogs played tag.
"If I were a dog, would you know it was me?" William Short
  asked his mother.
"Surely," said Mrs. Short.
  So William turned into a dog and frolicked and rollicked
  with the other dogs.
"I see you, William, dear," said his mother. "You're the only
  dog riding a tricycle."
"That's me," said William Short, and he gave a loud bark.

Near a puddle of mud the plump pigs dined.

"If I were a pig, would you know it was me?" William Short
asked his mother.

"I believe so," said Mrs. Short, opening the oven.

So William turned into a pig and snuffled and squealed with
the other pigs.

"I see you, William, dear," said his mother. "You're the only pig
who hasn't had lunch yet."

"That's me," said William Short,...

and he turned back into William Short with light brown hair,
dark blue eyes, and sneakers, and he walked into the kitchen
and had some lunch.